The Witch Goes F

Griselda the Gruesome – the oldest, meanest, wickedest witch in the world – cackled contentedly in her deck chair at the North Pole.

'What a wonderful holiday I'm having here at Iceberg Hotel,' she croaked. 'Perfect weather!' The blizzard got fiercer . . .

Also by Ralph Wright

The Witch's Big Toe

RALPH WRIGHT

The Witch
Goes For Gold

Illustrated by Eileen Browne

MAMMOTH

A Mammoth Paperback

THE WITCH GOES FOR GOLD

First published in Great Britain 1988
by Methuen Children's Books Ltd.
Paperback edition first published 1989
by Mammoth
Michelin House, 81 Fulham Road, London SW3 6RB
Text copyright © 1988 Ralph Wright
Illustrations copyright © 1988 Eileen Browne
Printed in Great Britain by
Cox & Wyman Ltd, Reading

ISBN 0 7497 0004 1

A CIP catalogue record for this title is available
from the British Library.

Contents

1 Griselda, the Champion . . .   7
  . . . and Wendy, the Challenger
2 Griselda Loses Her Temper . . .   19
  . . . and Wendy Has Yoghurt Trouble
3 A Gruesome Team . . .   32
  . . . and a Television Interview
4 On the Attack . . .   45
  . . . and Out on the Track
5 A Slip of the Cauldron . . .   61
  . . . and a Huddle of Witches
6 The As-You-Were Potion . . . 74
  . . . and the Witch Olympics
7 'Seventeen Times as High as the
  Moon'   88

1 · Griselda, the Champion . . .

Griselda the Gruesome – the oldest, meanest, wickedest witch in the world – cackled contentedly in her deck chair at the North Pole.

'What a wonderful holiday I'm having here at Iceberg Hotel,' she croaked. 'Perfect weather!' The blizzard got fiercer. A curious polar bear plodded up across the snow; but one snarl from Griselda was enough to scare it off.

Griselda snapped off an icicle from the brim of her witch's hat and gnawed at it, enjoying the happy thought that it would soon be time for the Witch Olympic Games. Time for her to collect another Gold Medal!

Not that Griselda was short of Gold Medals; she had twenty-five already! One for each of the last twenty-five Witch Olympics; and all her medals were for winning the Olympic Hexathlon.

(Other Olympics have a Pentathlon, which has five events, and a Decathlon, which has ten; but the Witch Olympics have the Hexathlon – *six* hard competitions all on the first day of the Games.)

Griselda was once the best in the world at all

the six events; but she grew lazy, and found it easier to win by cheating. And now she was 571 and beginning to get old, she'd found an even easier way to win the medal – by making sure no other witch went in for it.

It was hardly any trouble to scare them off. The last witch to challenge Griselda disappeared mysteriously, and the one before that had a nasty accident with her broomstick. Word soon got round that it was safer to go in for, say, the High-Dive-into-a-Hot-Cauldron Contest than to tackle Griselda, the Hexathlon Queen!

'Nobody will dare to challenge me this year,' gloated Griselda. She was probably right! It was the last day for entries, and no one had challenged her yet. 'Easy-freezy,' said Griselda. 'The medal's as good as mine!'

A horrible thought struck her. 'What if there *is* someone heading for the Witch Olympic Office right now, clutching a last-minute entry form?' This thought gave Griselda a nasty moment. Then, with an evil laugh, she reached under the deck chair for her Book of Spells.

She said:

> *'If there IS any witch set on taking MY place*
> *May her journey turn into an obstacle race!*
> *She'll be late for the deadline, and sunk*
> *   without trace!'*

'That ought to do it,' cackled Griselda, and went off to build a snow-witch.

. . . and Wendy, the Challenger

Wendy Witch was on her way to London, her entry form for the Witch Olympics tucked into the sleeve of her witch's gown, when she ran into a hot air balloon.

Head on!

One minute she was flying the broomstick without a care in the world; the next, there was

9

a strange sort of cackle of laughter, and she was sinking into the folds of this – whatever it was and the more Wendy and her broomstick struggled, the more the thing closed around them.

'What's this?' the young witch yelled. 'Is it some new kind of cloud? If so, it's the toughest kind of cloud I've ever come across! Why didn't you look where you were going, broomstick?'

'Why didn't you?' retorted the broomstick. '*You*'re the driver!'

'Miaow!' said Midnight, the witch's black cat, not wanting to be left out of the argument.

The truth was that they'd *all* been dozing in the warm sunshine, instead of hurrying on as they ought to have done; and now they might be too late!

Wendy kicked at the material as it tried to wrap itself round her legs.

'Who cackled, anyway? Did you cackle?' she asked the broomstick.

'*I* certainly didn't cackle,' said the broomstick. 'It must have been the cat.'

'Cats don't cackle,' Wendy objected. 'Do you cackle, Midnight?'

'Miaow,' said Midnight.

'See,' said Wendy, 'they don't. But somebody did.'

It was the Blue Witch's idea to put Wendy in for the 5,000-metre Broom Race. Wendy was so nippy on her broomstick, the old witch noticed, that she always beat the other witches to their batburger picnics at Witch's Hill, and was always first to the Witchcraftware Parties in the churchyard, even at dead of night. The Blue Witch was sure Wendy could do well in the race. And how nice it would be to see a witch from Willowdale in the Olympics! She'd be thrilled to coach Wendy for the race.

'Mind you,' she warned her, 'none of that mischievous magic of yours, that upsets everyone and causes so much trouble!' For the youngest witch in Willowdale was a fun-loving girl, and liked nothing better than to play alarming tricks on her friends with a comical spell or two. And even her helpful magic seemed to get out of hand . . .

Wendy was delighted at the Blue Witch's idea. 'Don't worry! I'll train hard, and I won't be any trouble – you'll see!'

They happened to tell the Grey Wizard their plan, and he had a shock for them.

'You'd better put a spurt on – it's the last day to enter!' he told them. There was nothing for it but to send Wendy off to London right away, and hope she could make it before the Witch Olympic Office closed.

Wendy set off in a rush, waving goodbye to the Blue Witch below, and made good speed – until she dozed off, and ended up running into that hot air balloon.

11

'Whatever this stuff is,' said Wendy Witch, still kicking and wriggling, 'we can't seem to get out of it. I shall have to make a spell.' After a moment's thought she said:

'Billowy cloud, or whatever you are,
I wish you were somewhere tremendously
FAR!'

'Oh, good,' said Sam Potts, standing in the basket below the hot air balloon. 'That bird that flew into my balloon seems to have gone. Now I can get back to business – which means travelling as far as I can to try and win the Long-Distance Balloon Race!' He looked down to see if he'd lost any height – and gulped! Where was the green English countryside? All he could see was a dry landscape of hot red dust and rock. A movement caught Sam's eye as something bounded across the plain beneath him.

'I don't believe it!' he whispered. 'It's – a kangaroo!'

Meanwhile Wendy was trying to make up for lost time. But the sky seemed very crowded today.

'Witches had an easier time of it in the old days,' she complained. 'The sky wasn't full of hazards then! Nowadays you've got to watch out for pylons – and electricity cables – and television transmitters – and radio masts – look out, broomstick – not to mention all this traffic that's whizzing about the sky today, from helicopters to hang-gliders!'

Wendy was soon quite worn out, dodging all the obstacles that seemed to fly into her path on purpose. After getting tangled up in someone's kite-string she realised she was so late now that there was hardly any chance of getting to London on time, unless she could find a way through this terrible traffic jam.

Just then, from the corner of her eye, the little witch glimpsed the nose of a large aeroplane. It had come up behind her unawares.

'That's just the sort of thing I mean,' said Wendy indignantly. 'Creeping up and making me jump like that! We witches were here first, you know!'

Then Wendy had an idea. 'Let's race the aeroplane, broomstick. It'll be good practice for the Olympics!'

In the cockpit the pilot was feeling relaxed as he scanned the blue sky around him.

'All clear to starboard,' he noted, 'witch on broomstick to port, weather fine ahead.' He gave a start. 'Did I say *witch* on *broomstick?* I'm seeing things!' But the dark figure was still there, its gown flapping. 'It really *is* a witch on a broomstick! What's more, she's flying faster than me!'

The pilot was proud of his plane. It was a

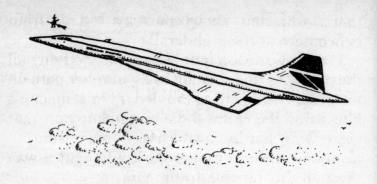

marvel of the latest technology. It was the best plane in the world, and wasn't he the best pilot? No scruffy witch was going to outfly *him!* He put on a burst of speed.

Wendy Witch looked over her shoulder.

'He's catching up,' she called. 'Faster, broomstick!' The broomstick surged forward. Midnight dug her claws into Wendy's shoulder and hung on.

The pilot couldn't believe his eyes. The witch was pulling ahead! He built up to top speed. The plane rattled and shook as it strained to beat Wendy Witch. Inside the cabin the poor passengers rattled and shook too. In spite of all the pilot could do, Wendy managed to keep that little bit ahead.

She giggled and said, 'Let's really give him something to think about, shall we, Midnight?'

Wendy looped the loop!

The pilot's mouth dropped open when he

14

saw this. Then he closed it with a snap and gritted his teeth.

'Right!' he decided. 'Anything you can do, *I* can do better.' He flicked a switch and the FASTEN YOUR SEATBELTS sign lit up in the cabin. He threw the plane into a steep climb – then flipped over and flew upside-down!

The passengers' stomachs lurched. Jenny, the air hostess, had just served the meals, but it wasn't the sight of the food which upset their insides; it was more the way their chicken dinners rose unsteadily from the trays, did forward rolls in the air, then dropped back into their laps, that made them feel queasy.

Wendy Witch clapped excitedly.

'It's just like the Red Arrows, isn't it, Midnight!' she said. 'I never thought a giant jet could do that.'

The pilot had forgotten all about his passengers. Now he only cared about beating the witch.

'If I can't fly faster than her – I bet I can fly *higher,*' he said. He worked his controls. The plane climbed.

Twenty thousand feet higher, the pilot levelled the plane. He looked carefully all round. Surely no broomstick could follow as high as this!

'I've beaten her this time!' he crowed.

But there was Wendy again – above him! To

the pilot's disgust she turned and gave him a friendly wave. His nostrils flared. His face began to twitch. Again he sent the plane up, higher than it had ever been before. But it was no good – there she was again, that infuriating witch, smiling and waving overhead! How did she do it?

'I give up!' screeched the pilot. 'All my expensive training – useless! My space-age electronics – junk! Couldn't even beat a kid on a piece of wood!' He shook his fist. He began to cry.

The plane nosed downwards. Out of sight of the pilot, Wendy landed on top of the fuselage.

'That was a fine idea of yours, broomstick, to hitch a lift on the plane's back each time it flew higher. I bet the pilot thought we got there all by ourselves!'

The crafty broomstick grinned. It had saved itself a lot of work! Even better, by hitching a ride on the plane they'd saved lots of time and landed early at London Airport. The passengers got out. 'What an exciting trip!' they were all saying. But some men in white coats came and took away the sobbing pilot.

'Poor man,' said Wendy, feeling sorry for him. 'I wonder what happened to upset him? Come on, broomstick, wake up. It's not far to the Witch Olympics office from here!'

The witch got there in good time and handed

in her entry form. But the wizard on duty said the Broom Race list was full already; the only event still open was the Hexathlon.

'The Hexathlon?' said Wendy. 'What's that?'

'It's all in the Rule Book,' said the wizard, giving her a booklet with the Witch Olympics design on it – crossed broomsticks with cat rampant. 'Do you want to go in for it or not?'

'Yes, please,' said Wendy. 'As long as I go in for something, the Blue Witch won't be disappointed.' So the wizard wished her luck at the Olympics in five weeks' time, and Wendy set off back to Willowdale.

'We're going to the Olympics, Midnight, we're really going to do it! Isn't it exciting?' said the little witch. Luckily there were no hold-ups on the journey back. At Wendy's house the Blue Witch was still waiting up anxiously. Wendy rushed in to tell her the good news.

'. . . only I had to go in for the Hexathlon instead,' explained Wendy. 'Whatever's the matter?'

The Blue Witch had gone pale. 'That's Griselda's event! She's not going to like this, you know! Not a bit!'

The television news was on: 'The Long-Distance Balloon Race was won today by Sam Potts,' said the newsreader. 'His balloon covered a sensational 12,000 miles, reaching

17

Australia. 'I don't know *how* it happened,' Sam
told reporters. 'Suddenly I was there – just like
magic!'

'Amazing!' said Wendy. 'However did he do
it?'

The Blue Witch had a sudden thought. 'You
did keep out of trouble today, like I said?
You're sure you didn't upset anyone?'

'Who, me?' said Wendy, innocently.

2 · Griselda Loses Her Temper . . .

At the North Pole, a little, pot-bellied, bald magician called Malicious paid for his ice cream and toddled back to his favourite iceberg. He got a surprise. A great, fat, flapping thing was sitting in his deck chair.

Was it a walrus?

Was it a whale?

No. It was Griselda the Gruesome, opening a letter from the Witch Olympic office.

As Malicious drew near, Griselda read the letter. Her eyes bulged. Her faced turned purple, with furious yellow spots round the edges. Sparks sprang from her bony fingertips.

'Someone has dared,' she spluttered, 'to challenge me in the Hexathlon competition after all! In spite of my spell! ME, the Hexathlon Queen! What impudent HUSSY could it be?' Griselda turned the page. There it was, the name of her challenger:

WENDY WITCH

The heat of Griselda's glare scorched the name on the paper until it first turned black, then burst into flames. Steam hissed from Griselda's ears. The ice melted round her deck chair until suddenly she was in a pool of icy water, and had to swim for it.

'Aagh!' Griselda shrieked, sizzling with fury as Malicious helped her out. 'I'll make you sorry for this, Sandy Witch, or whatever your name is!'

Malicious got her back to her hotel room at last, though she was three times his size. Inside Room 42, the magician got a fright. An enormous bat filled half the room!

Griselda hit it sharply with a stick, gazed into its eyes, and said, 'Show me that witch at once!'

To the magician's amazement, pictures appeared in the bat's sleepy eyes: pictures of Wendy and the Blue Witch practising for the Olympics.

'It's just like television!' he said.

'Shut up,' screeched Griselda. 'They've started training already! And that old one with the blue gown's put them on a special yoghurt diet. Yoghurt? I'll give you yoghurt, Brenda Witch!'

Cackling nastily, Griselda reached for her Book of Spells. Then she said:

'Fond of yoghurt? I'll make sure
You get a drop more than you bargained for!'

. . . and
Wendy Has Yoghurt Trouble

The Blue Witch found out all about the Hexathlon, and they got down to some hard work. Wendy practised the Broomstick Hurl until the poor broomstick was dizzy; then, while it recovered, she practised the Toad-and-Spoon Race, making the toad jump out of the spoon over and over again, until she could catch it before it hit the ground nearly every time. Even Midnight the cat was hard at work practising for the Witch's Cat Race. Of course the Blue Witch would be Wendy's partner in the Synchronized Broomstick Flying; but who would run with them in the Relay? They'd need two more witches to make up the team, and that was a problem; for everyone they asked was too afraid of Griselda.

'Never mind, Wendy, we'll find someone,' said the Blue Witch. 'They're right to be nervous; Griselda *will* try to stop us. She's at the North Pole just now, I've heard, but we must look out for trouble when she gets back!'

At the end of a week Wendy was stiff and sore from all the hard work.

'You deserve a day off, dear,' the Blue Witch told her. 'Go out with Jessica and enjoy

21

yourself. But will you get the broomstick seen to first? It's getting very sluggish.'

'Yes, it's time for its service. I'll see to it,' Wendy promised.

But when Wendy's friend Jessica came round next morning the witch was in a terrible state.

'I'm glad you've come!' gasped Wendy at the door. 'Come in and help me catch the broomstick!'

'What's the matter with it?' asked Jessica, as the broomstick dived past the two girls.

It flew upstairs, rattling the bannisters and banging the walls, wailing, 'I won't go! I *won't!*'

'It's got to go in for its 10,000-mile service at the garage, or it won't be in good shape for the Olympics in a month's time,' explained Wendy tearfully. 'But it doesn't want to go.'

'How would *you* like having your insides tampered with?' wailed the broomstick down the stairwell.

'It's all for your own good!' called Wendy. 'Better than having a breakdown in the middle of the Games!'

'I'm having a *nervous* breakdown already!'

'Poor thing!' said Jessica. 'It's frightened, that's all. Let *me* talk to it.'

Jessica went upstairs, spoke in a soothing voice to the broomstick, and soon they came down together arm in twig.

'I think it'll be okay now,' Jessica said. 'I've promised it a giant pot of yoghurt all to itself when it gets home.'

The Blue Witch's special yoghurt diet had proved a great success with the broomstick who couldn't get enough of it. Wendy stuck to the cobweb and bat's wool flavour, but the broomstick liked all kinds, and strawberry most of all. This was Jessica's favourite too.

Well, Jessica's calm words and the promised yoghurt worked wonders. The girls reached the garage after only a few more grumbles from the broomstick, and handed it over to Steve, the mechanic.

'Bye!' said Wendy with a lump in her throat. 'We'll collect you this afternoon.'

'What shall we do till then?' asked Jessica.

'I know! Let's go to the funfair at Poggleton Hall.'

So they got on the bus and sat upstairs at the front. Jessica unzipped her shoulder bag and took out a pot of yoghurt.

Wendy was so grateful to Jessica for helping with the broomstick that, after a minute's thought, she said:

> *'Jessica deserves a treat –*
> *All the yoghurt she can eat!'*

'That sounds like a spell,' said Jessica. How exciting it was that her school friend had turned into a witch!

'Of course it is,' said Wendy. 'All you have to do, when your yoghurt's empty, is say, "Flow, yoghurt, flow," and it'll fill again. But don't forget to say, "Stop, pot, stop," when you've had enough.'

Jessica was thrilled, and tried it at once. It almost overflowed before she remembered to say, 'Stop, pot, stop.'

'Thanks, Wendy. What a nice present! Oh, look – here we are already.'

The girls rushed off the bus. But when they got to the funfair Wendy didn't feel like any of the rides after all. She was too tired from her training.

'Can we go and see the Hall instead?' she asked Jessica. So they crossed the gravel forecourt of Poggleton Hall to the front entrance.

A jovial curator sold them two tickets to see round the stately home, and wished them a happy visit.

'Watch out for the ghost!' he warned merrily.

'Ooh! What ghost?' said both girls together.

'The ghost of Sir Thomas Poggleton, of course! They call him The Hungry Ghost because he stalks the Hall calling for his dinner – so they say. Not that I've ever seen him myself, but it might be *your* lucky day!'

Wendy and Jessica joined the guided tour. A group of sightseers stared disapprovingly at the girls.

'I'm surprised they allow *children* in here,' said one.

'They'll put sticky fingermarks on the paint-work,' sighed another.

'Children make such a noise,' a third shuddered.

'Well, *we* don't,' Wendy retorted indignantly. 'We're no trouble at all, are we, Jessica?'

'Can we get on, please?' said the guide.

They saw the Great Hall and the Parlour; they saw the Great Stairs with the hole in the bannister made by a cannonball; they saw the Great Dining Room, King Charles's Room, the Long Gallery, the Kitchen with its huge roasting spits, and the Servants' Hall; and about a million paintings of famous members of the Poggleton family through the ages.

After an hour Jessica whispered, 'Let's explore on our own – we might see the ghost!'

'All right,' the witch whispered back. Nobody noticed them slipping away. Seeing a staircase, the girls climbed till they found themselves in the attics. They searched room after room, finding lots of dust but no sign of the ghost; and finally Jessica flopped herself down on a window seat, disappointed.

'Now for some refreshments!' she said.

'What, again?' laughed Wendy, who was secretly glad they hadn't found the ghost.

Her friend got out the yoghurt pot.

'Flow, yoghurt, flow!' she said. As soon as the pot was brimful she tucked in. 'It still works!' she said, delighted.

Just then they heard a cackle of laughter, sounding quite clear and close, which made them clutch each other in fright.

'The ghost?' breathed Wendy.

'But where can it *be?*' said Jessica; and they peered round corners hoping to catch sight of it. But there was nothing to see; because the cackle had come on a breath of magic all the way from its real owner at the North Pole.

'We must have imagined it,' said Wendy at last. 'Anyway it's time to fetch the broomstick.'

'Did you see the ghost?' asked the curator on their way out.

'We thought we heard it,' said Wendy, 'but we must have been mistaken.'

And, as they walked to the bus stop, a small pot of yoghurt left behind in the attic, forgotten because of the mysterious cackle, began to overflow . . .

On the bus Wendy Witch worried about her broomstick. 'I shouldn't have left it. I should have stayed to hold its twigs and wipe its poor petrol tank! What a bad witch I am, to desert my broomstick in its hour of need!'

Jessica patted her arm. 'It'll be fine – you'll see!'

Back at Poggleton Hall, a glistening mound of yoghurt had filled the attic. The thick creamy stuff wobbled with each pink glob that dropped off the window seat. Soon a slow river of yoghurt reached the top of the back stairs. Then it slopped over the edge . . .

Wendy ran in to the garage. There was the broomstick, looking pale and wan.

'Oh!' Wendy Witch shrieked. 'What's happened to you? Are you all right, broomstick?'

The broomstick pointed an accusing finger at the mechanic. 'I'm lucky to be alive after what *he's* done to me! I had a complete blood transfusion . . .'

Steve spread his hands. 'An oil change, that's all, '' he explained.

'. . . and a heart transplant!'

'It was just a new water-pump!'

'It was torture!' groaned the broomstick.

'How could you be so cruel?' said Wendy, glaring at the mechanic, and stomped off outside with the broomstick, leaving her friend to thank Steve and pay the bill.

Outside Jessica had to comfort them both. 'There, there,' she told the broomstick. 'It wasn't so bad, was it? Have you forgotten the yoghurt I promised?' The broomstick perked up at once.

But when she searched her bag, Jessica gave a cry. 'It's gone! I must have left it behind at the Hall!'

'Don't worry,' said Wendy. 'As long as you remembered to say, ''Stop, pot, stop'' . . .'

'But I didn't!' groaned Jessica. Wendy stared at her in horror.

'Come on!' yelled the witch, grabbing her broomstick. 'Climb on, Jessica. We must get back to the Hall right away!'

'Ow!' howled the broomstick. 'I've just had a critical operation. I need weeks of intensive care!'

'Oh, shut up!' said the little witch, forgetting all her sympathy of a moment ago. 'This is an emergency. We could have a major disaster on our hands!'

They got there much quicker by broom than by bus, and soon landed in front of Poggleton Hall. What a sight they saw!

Great pink waterfalls of yoghurt gushed down into the forecourt from the upstairs windows. Fountains of yoghurt jetted out of the chimneys. Sprays of it gleamed in the sunshine before spattering down on the roof. It hung in wobbly stalactites from the gargoyles. Mounds of it lay around the gardens, lapped at by a delighted army of cats and dogs.

Wendy rushed to the entrance. But just then the main doors sprang open and a huge tidal wave of yoghurt poured out. The forecourt became a pink sea.

Tempting red lumps of strawberry floated past. Then came all the people, swept out of the Hall by the flood of yoghurt. The girls waved as the curator floated by, pink to the tips of his ears.

'Strawberry! My favourite!' he called to them happily.

Next came the sightseers from the guided tour, who'd been so unfriendly to the two girls. They surged past, up to their middles in yoghurt. They seemed awfully cross.

'I don't think strawberry can be *their* favourite,' Wendy decided.

The witch found a way inside through an attic window, and they raced through yoghurt-

soaked rooms on the broomstick until they reached the one with the yoghurt pot in it.

'Stop, pot, stop!', they cried, and at last the little plastic volcano stopped erupting.

Then they heard a burp, and turned to see someone in the corner of the room, dipping into a huge heap of yoghurt with a silver spoon. A satisfied smile lit up his face. It was a big bearded man, strangely dressed in doublet and hose, with a feathered cap on his head and a short sword hanging at his hip.

He beamed at the girls. 'Enough to eat at last!' he rumbled, dipping in for another enormous helping. 'Now I can rest in peace!' He stood up and patted his bulging belly happily. 'No more shall I haunt Poggleton Hall!' he cried, turning on his heel and walking out of the room.

'Well, that's someone who's happy, at least,' smiled Wendy. 'They don't seem too pleased down there.' Shrill cries of rage rose from the forecourt, where people struggling out of the sticky yoghurt kept slipping and falling in again. Wendy sighed. 'It'll take a whole week's supply of magic to clear up this mess. Who d'you think that man was, Jessica?'

Jessica's eyes were wide. 'It was the ghost, of course! Sir Thomas Poggleton, the Hungry Ghost! Only he's not hungry any more – thanks to you, Wendy!'

But the witch had fainted, toppling off the broomstick right into the sticky heap of yoghurt.

'I think I'm going *off* yoghurt a bit,' said Jessica.

3 · A Gruesome Team . . .

Gazing gleefully into the enormous bat's eyes, Griselda saw it all. She watched in fits of laughter as Wendy had to waste all her precious magic clearing up Poggleton Hall, instead of using it to practise her Olympic skills.

'Everything's going to plan!' the old witch jeered. 'From now on it'll get even tougher, Glenda Witch. I'll see you never make it to the Olympics! You'll wish you'd never tangled with the Hexathlon Queen!'

Malicious the Magician was snoring quietly in a corner of the room. Griselda had forgotten all about him in her delight at Wendy's misfortunes. Now she woke him up with a hefty kick.

The two of them got chatting.

Griselda soon found that Malicious was nearly as mean, cruel, deceitful, spiteful, and nasty as *she* was. It was hate at first sight.

'You're just my kind of person!' she croaked. 'Why don't we get married?'

Dodging the witch's bad breath, Malicious agreed at once.

They were married next day by the dread Ice Queen, who was in charge of such things at the North Pole. Her icy breath chilled even the cold hearts of Malicious and Griselda.

'Do you, Malicious, promise to obey Griselda in all things without answering back?'

'I don't like the sound of that . . .' Malicious protested. But a sudden, agonising pain shot up his leg. Griselda was treading on his toe!

'Promise, promise!' screeched Griselda.

'. . . and above all, do you promise to help her defeat the young upstart, Wendy Witch?'

'Oh, all right then,' sighed Malicious, rubbing his toe. 'I do.'

'I now pronounce you magician and wife!' said the Ice Queen.

The happy couple went straight to Room 42 to pack.

'Where shall we go on our honeymoon, my dear Griselda?' said Malicious. 'Or may I call you Gristle for short, now we're married?'

'Honeymoon?' shrieked Griselda. 'What honeymoon? We're off to Willowdale, of course, to finish off that impudent little Mandy Witch!'

She thumped the bat, to find out what Wendy was up to. To Griselda's disgust the little witch was excitedly getting ready to be interviewed on television! Griselda snorted and reached for her Book of Spells.

'I'll make such a fool of her that she'll give up her Olympic plans! Here's just what I need: a Go Wrong spell . . .

> *I'll spoil your day by magic skill –*
> *Whatever CAN go wrong – it WILL!'*

Griselda packed her Book of Spells away in her suitcase along with her other favourites: *Famous Broomsticks of the Olympics, Superwitch: The Hexathlon Queen* (which was all about herself) and an exciting thriller called *Hex Marks the Spot*. On second thoughts she kept the thriller out to read on the way; it would be a long, hard journey to Willowdale.

. . . and a Television Interview

'Only three weeks to the Olympics now,' said the Blue Witch, 'and so much to do! We can't afford any more disasters, Wendy, if we're to be ready for the Games on time. This habit of yours – letting your magic get out of hand, causing no end of trouble – it'll have to stop!''

Wendy looked crestfallen. 'I don't *mean* to do

it,' she explained, 'it just seems to happen! I'll try to do better, I really will.'

'I'm sure you will, dear,' said the Blue Witch kindly. 'At least your broomstick's running smoothly now, so we can work on that Double Backward Swoop till we get it just right. First thing tomorrow, then?'

'Right!' said Wendy eagerly. 'And Midnight's looking forward to her early morning jog, too!' She gave the little black cat a hug as the Blue Witch got up to go.

So breakfast was early next day at the witch's house. Only munching and slurping noises could be heard. The munching was Wendy eating her Shredded Weevils, and Midnight eating *her* favourite cereal, Miaowsli. The disgusting slurping noise was the broomstick's fault. Wendy was just going to tell it to eat its yoghurt more politely, when the telephone rang.

'This is the television speaking,' said a voice.

'Don't be silly,' replied Wendy. 'It's switched off, I can see it from here. *You* mean, it's the telephone speaking!'

After a long pause the voice said, 'Who am I speaking to?'

'How should I know?' Wendy answered. 'I can't see who's there with you.'

'All I'm trying to say,' said the voice, beginning to sound quite ill, 'is that I'm Perry Logan, the television reporter, you know, and I want to interview the famous Witch Olympics Hexathlete, Wendy Witch!'

'Oh, I see!' said Wendy, getting excited.

'Well, can we come round to do the interview – about six o'clock?'

'Yes! Yes, of course,' Wendy said breathlessly.

Almost at once the Blue Witch roared to a halt outside – on a brand new De Luxe Hatchback Supabroom.

'I bought it specially for the Olympics,' she told Wendy proudly. 'But what wonderful news! You're to be on television!'

'Isn't it exciting?' said Wendy, giving the wrinkled old witch a hug in the hall. 'But how did you know?'

'By magic, of course. What's the use of being a witch unless you can be first to pick up the gossip? Forget the training for today – we must have you looking your best for the interview. What will you be wearing?'

'My best gown, I suppose. Oh, dear, it needs a wash – it's still covered with yoghurt!' Wendy fetched her gown and stuffed it in the washing machine, leaving it open in case she thought of anything else. Just then she heard a cackle of laughter – just the one she and Jessica had heard at the Hall. Wendy went to tell the Blue Witch about it; but she was astonished to find the old witch and the broomstick doing a mad dance together round the coffee table, singing, 'We'll win the Hexathlon!' Round and round they span.

Crash! The hard end of the broomstick hit poor Wendy in the mouth.

'Ooh!' moaned the witch. 'You've knocked all my teeth out!' She ran to the mirror. The old witch and the broomstick peered over her shoulders.

'Don't exaggerate,' said the broomstick. 'You've only chipped a bit off *one*.'

'But it looks awful!' Wendy wailed. 'I can't possibly go on television now.'

'Yes you can,' said the Blue Witch briskly. 'I'll ring the dentist at once. He'll cap the tooth for you. You'd better have your hair done too. I'll ring the Grey Wizard's Hair Salon.'

'That's lucky,' she said finally. 'The dentist can see you at once, and the Grey Wizard can fit you in this afternoon. Come on then!'

At the gate, Wendy remembered the washing machine. To save her going back in, she made a quick spell:

'Washing machine – start up and spin
So my gown's ready for when I come in!'

In the kitchen the washer obligingly shut its door and began. How was Wendy to know Midnight the cat had crawled inside for a nap?

Mr Preece was a very careful dentist and hardly ever hurt. Wendy needed a filling, too, he found when he looked in her mouth. So he gave her an injection and she never even noticed. But Wendy was a terrible coward in the dentist's chair. As soon as she heard the drill whirring she panicked and said:

'How I hate that dentist's drill –
Make the horrid thing be still!'

The spell worked in a curious way: the drill stopped – but Mr Preece began to spin instead! He pirouetted; he revolved merrily. Sunlight reflected off his glasses, one flash for every turn, like a lighthouse. Wendy sat fascinated.

Mary, the nurse, came in. 'Oh!' she gasped. 'What's that – a whirlwind? A tornado? Where's Mr Preece?'

'That *is* Mr Preece,' explained Wendy.

Mary took a closer look at the whirling dentist. 'He's never done this kind of thing before. Are you sure?' Then a strangled cry of 'help' came from the spinning column.

'Yes – that's his voice all right,' nodded Mary, and began to sob. 'Poor, kind Mr Preece! To think it should come to this. Never again to hear his cheery "rinse out!" or his "this won't hurt a bit!"'

Wendy patted her arm. 'It's not as bad as all that,' she tried to say, 'I'll think of another spell,' but the words came out all jumbled and funny. Whatever was wrong?

Of course! The injection was starting to work, making her mouth numb. And because she couldn't say the words properly, the spell wouldn't work! She tried one, but it was hopeless.

Such an awful thing hadn't happened to Wendy since she was at Witch's School. She was so upset she threw her arms round Mary and both of them sobbed together.

Mr Preece continued to whirl.

'Oh, look!' said Mary at last. 'Dear Mr

Preece is spinning so fast that he's drilling a hole in the floor.'

'So he is,' mumbled Wendy as sawdust sprayed the room.

'He's drilling his last cavity!' wailed Mary.

The dentist sank lower into the floor and finally dropped right through the ceiling of the waiting room below, where the Blue Witch was sitting in a swivel chair. The others rushed downstairs.

Mr Preece landed in the Blue Witch's lap. The swivel chair swivelled madly.

The Blue Witch shrieked and kicked a lot until she recovered from her surprise. Luckily *her* mouth wasn't numb, so she said:

> *'Whoever you are that came down from above*
> *Do my poor knees a favour: keep still, would you,*
> *love?'*

To everyone's relief, the swivel chair stopped. Mr Preece took off his glasses and rubbed his eyes.

'I must have had a dizzy spell!' he said.

'You certainly did,' said Wendy; though the words came out funny again.

So the Blue Witch saved the day; and the kindly dentist, in spite of his ordeal, finished the job. Soon Wendy left, with teeth as even as ever.

'Now for your hair!' said the old witch.

The Grey Wizard's Hair Salon was the sensation of the month. Just a shake of the wizard's wand, and any style you fancied could be yours in a trice! Wendy sat down to pick one from the photos in the wizard's Hairstyle Album.

Which to choose? Merlin's Beard? The Gorgeous Gorgon, with its plaits like writhing snakes? The Magic Mohican, perhaps? The prettiest was one called EnchanTresses, Wendy decided. But maybe Siren's Swirls or Witch's Waves would suit her better? Certainly not the Wet Seaweed Look, or the Hag-in-a-Hurricane!

'Ah, it's young Wendy, our very own Olympic athlete!' said the Grey Wizard. 'We'll all be cheering for you! I'll be there myself, you know, as a referee. But what can I do for you today? How about my newest styles: Dragged-Through-a-Hedge-Backwards, and Dragged-Through-a-Hedge-Forwards. What do you think – exciting, eh?'

Wendy shook her head very hard, and pointed instead to Siren's Swirls.

And the wizard was exactly halfway through the wave of his wand when his young customer jumped up with a horrified expression on her face. She rushed out of the Salon, dragging the surprised Blue Witch along behind her.

For the little witch had had a sudden thought:

where's Midnight got to? And in a flash she remembered seeing her out of the corner of an eye – crawling into the washer!

Well, Midnight wasn't drowned. They found her looking reproachfully out of the porthole, as if to say, 'How *could* you?' A very bedraggled cat was quickly rescued – and stalked off with her nose in the air, still staggering from that final spin.

'Everyone's been in a spin today,' the Blue Witch remarked. 'First me and the broomstick, dancing, then the dentist, then me again in that swivel chair, and now poor Midnight in the washer!'

'Mm!' Wendy agreed.

'And you'll be in a spin, too, Wendy, if you don't get your best gown on. It'll soon be time for the television people to arrive!'

There was barely time to get the gown dry – then they discovered all the holes Midnight's claws had torn in it in the washing machine!

The television cameras arrived to find their star performer in a dress full of rips and her hair done on one side only (the other side was just like that Wet Seaweed Look). Worse was to come when the interview began.

'Tell me, Miss Witch – just how exciting *is* it to be entering for the Hexathlon this year? And how do you rate your chances of beating the mighty Griselda?' asked Perry Logan.

'Grooh!' said Wendy, her whole face numb from the injection. And, for the whole interview, that was all poor Wendy could say!

4 · On the Attack . . .

'Another disastrous day for Linda Witch!' gloated Griselda the Gruesome, watching the interview on television. The odious pair were resting. After the long journey to Willowdale on the back of the enormous black bat, they had booked into the Honeymoon Suite at Willowdale Motel, just in time for the Perry Logan show.

'I made a fool of her all right,' Griselda chortled. 'My Go Wrong spell worked perfectly. Now she's bound to pull out of the competition and my Hexathlon Gold will be safe.'

'Suppose she doesn't, though?' Malicious ventured.

His wife glared at him. 'Don't be a ninny! Of course she will.'

'She doesn't strike me as a giving-up sort of person, that's all,' the magician persisted. 'What if – I mean, what I had in mind –'

'Go on! What are you blithering on about?' snapped Griselda.

The magician pouted. 'Well – can't *I* have a go?'

'Well, well! So you want to be some use at last, do you? Well, why not? It's about time.' To show she was pleased Griselda gave her husband a hefty biff on the bald patch.

Soon the beastly twosome were airborne over Willowdale, searching for the little shop where, as the bat's wonderful eyes revealed, Wendy had gone to be alone after the interview.

'There it is!' screeched Griselda, spotting the name **W. Witch & Cat Ltd** over a shop in the High Street. They swooped down and landed outside. A poster in the window said: BAR-GAIN – ONE WEEK ONLY – HALF-PRICE BROOMSTICK RIDES.

'Now!' shrieked the crone. 'Do it now, Delicious!'

'Very well, my dear,' said Malicious. 'You know you can rely on me. But I wish you'd get *my* name right – I'm your husband after all.'

With an evil leer Malicious flourished his magic wand. The shop should have disappeared in a puff of smoke. But nothing happened.

'What is it? What's the matter?' the witch screamed.

The puzzled magician examined his wand.

'It must be the batteries,' he mumbled. 'The batteries in my wand have run out!'

'You gnat-brained numskull!' stormed Griselda. 'You bungling blockhead! You dithering dimwit . . .'

Wendy heard the commotion and came out of the shop.

'Hello, Griselda!' she exclaimed. 'And Malicious too! How nice! Won't you come in – you could give me some tips on the Hexathlon.'

'Tips?' fumed Griselda 'Here's a tip for you: give it up! Forget it!'

'Oh, I can't do that,' replied Wendy. 'Not after all the hard training I've done.'

Griselda shook her fist. 'You'll find it harder than you think from now on!' And she said:

> *'Venture on the running track –*
> *Problems three will hold you back*
> *Very soon your nerve will crack!'*

and with a cackle of evil laughter the loathsome pair flew away.

Wendy was impressed. 'A three-line spell!' she said. 'That's very powerful. I'd better watch out.' She went back into her Magic Spells shop, Griselda's cackle ringing in her ears. And suddenly she remembered where she'd heard that laugh before!

. . . and Out on the Track

'No wonder there were so many obstacles on

my way to London!' said Wendy, remembering all her troubles. 'No wonder we left the magic yoghurt pot behind! No wonder my television appearance went wrong! It was all Griselda's doing. The evil old crone! Well, I shan't give up! I'll fight you all the way, Griselda, you old cheat!'

Wendy put up a notice in the shop window: *Closed for the Witch Olympics,* and flew home in a much more cheerful mood.

'I can't wait to tell the Blue Witch about this,' she said. 'Our troubles weren't *my* fault after all – what a relief!'

Next morning the young witch put on a tracksuit instead of her witch's gown. 'I'll do a long run in the park. When the Blue Witch gets back, she'll be surprised how fit I am! And if I meet Griselda's "problems three" – well, I'll solve them, that's all!'

The witch jogged down the road, round the corner, turned left into Park Road – and she met her first problem. A big removal van stood in the road, with furniture scattered all around it. The road was completely blocked!

'Hello, Wendy,' said a man in a yellow hat nearby.

'How do you know my name?' asked Wendy.

'Saw you on television,' said the man. 'Your voice is different though.'

48

'Please don't mention that,' shuddered the witch.

'I'm having a bit of trouble moving house,' said Yellow Hat. 'Won't all go in the van, you see.' He waved at his furniture spread across the road. 'Got a spell to help me?'

'Certainly,' said Wendy. She said:

> *'Your furniture's too tall to fit.*
> *Here's the answer – shorten it!'*

Yellow Hat laughed to see his furniture shrink. It would fit a doll's house now! The removal man who was loading Yellow Hat's furniture picked up a piano *and* a wardrobe in one hand.

'Soon fit this lot in now, mate,' he said. 'Where's my assistant, Kevin? That lad's always sloping off when there's work to do! Kevin?'

Everyone looked about for Kevin. Something tugged at the leg of Wendy's tracksuit. Looking down, she saw a tiny little man. Wendy was excited. It must be a pixie – or an elf – or a leprechaun! She picked him up gently in the palm of her hand.

'Who *are* you?' she asked, noticing the big red buckles on his pointed shoes.

'I'm Kevin, you twerp!' squeaked the little fellow, glaring at her. 'You shrunk me with the furniture. I've nearly been trodden on twice! Just get me back to normal size quick!'

Hastily Wendy grew Kevin again while the men had a good laugh.

'Good luck in the Witch Olympics, Wendy!' they said. 'We'll be on your side!'

'Thank you,' said the witch, pleased. Now

the furniture was tiny Wendy could get past easily, and made her way into the park, where there was a running track. Wendy ran one lap. There was a lot of noise, as the Willowdale Show was being held in the park, and farm animals waited in their pens nearby for farmers to buy and sell them. The noise didn't worry Wendy. She imagined it was the Olympic crowd cheering as she ran in the Witch's Relay! Then on Wendy's next lap she met her second problem.

A massive bull stood astride the track!

Wendy eyed the bull's horns. The bull eyed the witch's hat and decided to take a friendly bite at it. Wendy squealed and backed away.

'Hey – you there!' came a voice. 'It's Wendy Witch, isn't it? I saw you on television!' The man was a farmer in check jacket, cap, and enormous boots. '. . . only I've just bought this bull at the Show. He's a stubborn one, we can't get him in the transporter. What we need's a spot of magic – if you've got the time, Miss?'

'All right,' said Wendy, sighing. When *was* she going to get on with her running? The farmer brought up his big truck. His men came up to push the bull, and pull him with ropes, but the bull, a handsome, massive fellow called Cuddles, took no notice of them. Funny little two-legged things, always in a hurry! It was a nice park; he liked it here. He decided to stay a bit longer. He looked at Wendy with interest. Pity she'd stopped running, thought Cuddles, it would have been fun to join in!

Wendy Witch said to the bull:

> *'To drag your feet is just not fair*
> *So I shall make you light as air!'*

'Hold on to those ropes!' Wendy called as Cuddles's feet left the ground. Now he was so light that only a shove was needed to start him drifting into the truck like a vast balloon. The tailgate crashed into place; the bolts slammed home. Cuddles was astounded. He had an idea he'd been tricked somehow, so he bellowed and snorted a bit; but really this weightless feeling was very enjoyable! Like being an astronaut! Did they have any astronaut jobs for bulls, he wondered?

'Remember, don't let him out till the magic's worn off,' the witch warned. She felt sorry for the bull – he'd only wanted a few minutes of freedom!

'Thanks for your help, Wendy,' the farmer said. 'I'll be cheering for you at the Olympics!' He drove the truck away to the village of Drowsy Hollow where he lived and, in half an hour, swung in through the farmyard gate.

There an eager farmhand rushed forward to open the back of the truck –

'Don't do that!' yelled the farmer.

Too late! Cuddles drifted out, light as a feather, and floated up into the sky. A breeze wafted him gently back towards Willowdale . . .

Wendy, meanwhile, had run three laps and was feeling pleased with herself. If there were no more interruptions she still had time for a good work-out. She put on speed.

Just then a plump policeman stepped out on to the track, waving his arms. He was right in Wendy's path and she couldn't stop. They collided and fell sprawling.

'P.C. Trunch!' Wendy puffed. 'Whatever are you up to?'

The policeman got up and dusted himself off.

'I need your help, Wendy,' he began. 'There's a thief in the park, snatching people's money. Already he's snatched Granny Baxter's handbag with all her snooker winnings in it; and he snatched Simon Snodgrass's pocket money right out of his hand, just as he was paying for an ice cream! It's a tricky case,' P.C. Trunch went on, 'but with *your* magic and *my* brilliant detective work, we could catch him in no time!'

'All right,' sighed Wendy. Another interruption! But she began to think hard about how she could help P.C. Trunch. 'This calls for a good disguise,' she said. 'I'll meet you here in twenty minutes.'

Wendy ran all the way home, and then all the

way back again dressed as a tree! It had cardboard branches, and paper leaves – and even a rather squashed partridge in it, for the tree costume was left over from Jessica's Fancy Dress Christmas party. The broomstick laughed several of its twigs off when Wendy put on her disguise, and decided to come along too, not to miss any of the fun.

Wendy stood as still as she could and tried to look like a tree. She'd put a tempting, fat purse on the path, feeling sure the Snatcher would come for it if he thought no one was there but a small tree. P.C. Trunch went off to do his detecting. Wendy waited and waited, but nobody came.

The witch began to get stiff and cold. It began to drizzle! Her leaves were getting soggy. She wanted to go home for a warm beside her electric storage cauldron. She felt quite weary and closed her eyes for a second.

The Snatcher struck!

He flitted silently out of a clump of rhododendrons, hooked up the purse with a deft hand, and fled.

Someone tubbier dropped out of his hiding place in a horse chestnut tree, and gave chase.

Wendy opened her eyes –

She saw the purse gone –

She spotted a running figure –

So she made a quick spell:

54

'No need for a tussle –
You cannot move a muscle!'

It worked! The figure froze like a statue.
'I've done it! I caught the Snatcher!' crowed
the little witch. 'Come on, broomstick, let's see
who it is.'

'Ahem,' it coughed. The broomstick had seen it all.

'There's something familiar about his back,' said Wendy. 'I feel sure it's someone we know!'

'Excuse me . . .' said the broomstick.

'P.C. Trunch *will* be pleased,' said Wendy, reaching her captive.

'Don't count on it,' murmured the broomstick.

'Oh, crumpets! It *is* P.C. Trunch!' gulped Wendy.

'I was trying to tell you,' sighed the broomstick.

'And the thief's got clean away! The purse had my earwig sandwiches in it too!' wailed the witch. The broomstick grinned.

'. . . *and* your yoghurt!' The broomstick scowled. 'Hadn't you better set the constable free?' it suggested.

Wendy looked miserable. 'He isn't going to be pleased! Oh, well – better get it over with.'

What a telling-off poor Wendy got when she freed P.C. Trunch from the Statue spell. What seemed to upset him most was the way his nose had itched just when he couldn't scratch it!

'Sorry,' said Wendy sheepishly. 'Sorry, P.C. Trunch! But don't worry – I've got just the thing to catch the Snatcher next time. I'll fetch it from my Magic Spells shop.'

Wendy ran all the way to her shop in the

High Street, and then she ran all the way back. She showed the policeman a packet of magic powder, just arrived from her Spells Catalogue.

SLOW-MOTION
ACTION-REPLAY POWDER
(As seen on television)
If Life is Passing You By . . .
Slow It Down with Our Wonderful Powder!
Gives You Time to Catch Up!

'. . . a dusting of this and he won't get away so easily!' explained Wendy.

'I don't think we'll get a chance to use it,' said P.C. Trunch gloomily. 'I'd say we've seen the last of the Snatcher for today!'

But he was wrong.

The Snatcher had lost his way in the trees, and suddenly he appeared on the path right next to them. He was wearing a mask – but Wendy's sharp eyes spotted something else.

'I know those shoes!' shrieked Wendy. 'It's Kevin!'

Kevin was horrified to see the policeman. He dashed between the pair and sprinted up the path – towards the removal van.

P.C. Trunch and Wendy followed – but only in slow motion. For when Kevin pushed between them he'd knocked the packet of magic slow-motion powder all over them both!

Cuddles the bull was having the time of his life. He'd never specially wanted to go ballooning or hang-gliding; it's not the sort of idea that usually crosses a bull's mind. But now he'd tried it, he was all for it. What an adventure! They'd never believe it back in the cowsheds!

But Cuddles was very slowly, an ounce at a time, getting his weight back. He was falling towards Willowdale. Where would he land? Not on top of that tower block, he hoped. Imagine a bull coming down all those stairs! Not in the shopping precinct . . . he was sure there'd be a butcher there, and he didn't fancy *that* at all! With a bit of luck it might be the park . . .

The escaping removal van had only got to the end of Park Road when Cuddles landed on top of it. It was a gentle landing, but the bull's great weight was now coming back so fast that the van ground to a halt, and slowly began to crumple.

Wendy and P.C. Trunch had to run as hard as they could just to move an inch at a time up the path.

'Griselda's ''problems three'' have beaten me after all,' fretted the young witch. 'I meant to spend all day running, and look what's happened instead!'

'Don't be silly,' said the plump policeman,

puffing hard. 'You've been running about all day. Didn't you run home for your disguise, and into town for the magic powder? And you're still running! This slow-motion running will be as good as fifty laps round the track by the time we get there!'

'You're right!' said Wendy, a happy smile spreading over her face. 'I shall be fit after all: I feel as fit as a flea already!'

Much slow-motion running later, they reached the scene in time to see Cuddles, tired but happy from his exciting day, taken away to safety, looking very proud of himself. The rescue services had already prised Kevin, the Snatcher, out of the crushed cab, and taken him and his loot into custody.

'That bull would make a good copper, the way he catches villains!' laughed Inspector Whistle. 'Let's recruit him into the Force!'

'What rank?' wondered P.C. Trunch.

'Chief Constabull! What else?'

5 · A Slip of the Cauldron . . .

A small black raincloud followed Wendy all the way home. It stayed high in the sky until the young witch closed the front door behind her. Then it plummeted down to land on the roof. The 'raincloud' split into three: Griselda, large and fat; the magician, thin but pot-bellied; and the enormous bat, which sat down to wait patiently by the chimney.

Malicious tottered along the ridge of the roof carrying a big cauldron. It was so heavy that he puffed and grunted, and looked likely to fall off at any moment. But he reached the gable end above Wendy's front door, where he sat down hard and wiped his brow on the sleeve of his robe.

Griselda perched beside him. This trouble-some Wendy Witch! She just wouldn't give up, in spite of the problems Griselda kept putting in her way.

'My spell stopped her training all right, but she spent all day running about helping people, and that gave her all the exercise she needed.

Helping people indeed!' Griselda snorted. 'There was no such nonsense in my young days. Cheating, turning people into toads, and giving them boils on the neck – that was always good enough for me!'

'Quite right, dear,' agreed her husband. 'Helping people is most unfair!'

'It's time for more drastic action,' said Griselda, smirking at the sight of the cauldron, full to the brim with Vanishing Powder. 'This lot will be enough to send her to Vanishing Land for years,' she gloated, 'long after the Hexathlon Gold is mine again!' She cackled so spine-chillingly that even the pigeons on the roof shuddered.

'Vanishing Land?' said Malicious. 'Where's that?'

'Don't you know?' said Griselda. 'It's the place where lost things go. Lost scarves and pens and hats and umbrellas; lost instructions for putting things together; lost homework, oodles and oodles of it; lost pencils, and dogs, and explorers; and of course, all those people who said: ''Come on – I know a really good short cut!'''

'But Wendy Witch isn't lost,' Malicious pointed out.

'Not yet she isn't,' Griselda cackled. 'But with a helping hand from this Vanishing Powder –'

Inside, Wendy had heard mysterious banging and clattering noises on her roof, so she put down her book, *Useful Olympic Spells,* and went out the front door to investigate.

Griselda spotted her below.

'There she is!' the crone shrieked. 'Tip the cauldron NOW, Malodorous!'

The magician paused and looked annoyed. 'Malicious is my name, not Malodorous! Do you know what Malodorous means? It means smelly. Smelly! That's not a nice thing to call a person at all. You're always getting my name wrong.'

But Griselda wasn't listening to her husband's complaints. She was beside herself with rage at the thought of Wendy escaping.

'Button it up, you old goat, and do it *now,* before she gets away!' she screamed, giving him an impatient shove.

At this the magician, who'd stood up, lost his footing on the tiles and managed to tip the cauldron backwards so that the powder went all over the enormous black bat. It vanished with a dull pop!

Griselda could hardly believe it. It was a total disaster! For several minutes she couldn't say a word, and just stared at Malicious in speechless horror.

In the end she whispered, 'How shall we get home now? We can't fly without the bat! And

perhaps you'll tell me how we get down from this roof?'

It was Wendy who came to their rescue. She fetched a ladder, then watched the shifty pair warily as they scrambled down.

'What *are* you up to, you two?' she asked. But they scuttled off down the road, never looking Wendy in the eye!

After this, Griselda had a dreadful tantrum lasting most of a week. Malicious spent a lot of time under the bed in the Honeymoon Chalet.

It was the only safe place as yells, curses, dishes and plates whizzed about the room.

When she ran out of crockery Griselda said, 'Here's one last chance for you to get things right. I have a new plan! Get up and listen carefully . . .'

. . . and a Huddle of Witches

'If I don't have some fun today, I'll burst!' said Wendy Witch, leaping out of bed one morning just a week before the Games. 'All these weeks of hard training, doing only kind, helpful magic to keep out of trouble – the strain's too much!' She was dressed in a trice, in her brightest orange and pink witch's gown.

She knocked on the Blue Witch's bedroom door.

'I'm going out,' she called. 'I don't feel like training today.'

'I'd better come with you. We agreed to stick together in case Griselda tries anything, didn't we? That's why I moved into your house!'

But Wendy didn't want that! 'Sybil and her friends will be here soon. Won't you stay and let them in?' The Blue Witch's old friend, Sybil Soreboils, who wasn't afraid of anybody – certainly not that Griselda the Gruesome – was coming to join Wendy.

'All right,' sighed the Blue Witch. 'But be careful! You'll be back by eleven o'clock to meet them, won't you?'

'Of course,' promised Wendy, and rushed downstairs. 'Come on, broomstick, let's go and have some fun!'

'Watch out,' warned the broomstick. 'You know that when you do *bad* magic, it ends with you getting the worst of it yourself.'

'I don't care. It'll be worth it!' Wendy replied, and began whistling happily.

But a little pot-bellied man disguised as a balloon seller smiled as he spotted her coming into town.

'She's out alone at last!' he chuckled. 'Now to keep her busy as long as I can.'

'What lovely balloons!' said the witch. 'I must have one of those.' She climbed off the broomstick and hurried up to the balloon seller; but he scuttled off down the street and turned in a doorway, his silver and blue balloons bobbing after him. 'That's strange,' thought Wendy, and followed him.

She found herself in the Town Hall! It was full of people, but none of them looked like the balloon seller. Wendy sat down to get her breath back, and noticed Perry Logan, the television presenter, on the stage.

'The seven finalists for the Miss Willowdale Beauty Contest have now been chosen, ladies and gentlemen,' said Perry. 'And now it's time to meet the lovely girls and ask each of them a question or two. Will the lucky seven come out on stage, please!'

'I'll have some fun with this Beauty Contest – you'll see!' Wendy whispered to the broomstick. She giggled and said:

'What a laugh – I'd be in stitches
If the finalists were WITCHES!

The loud applause from the audience turned to gasps of surprise when seven witches trooped out on stage! Wendy got a surprise, too – it was Sybil Soreboils and her friends. They must have been on their way to Wendy's house when the spell brought them here. There was Peg Pigbristle and Norabel Knockaknees; there was Tabitha Toothlesscrone and Winifred Wart; and hobbling behind them came Sybil with Harriet Horsefeatures and little Bathsheba Bogdribbling.

They hadn't expected to be in a beauty contest, but now they *were,* the witches were happy to play their part. With whoops and shrieks the crones skipped to the front of the stage. A shower of frogs and lizards escaped from Tabitha's tattered gown. An evil-smelling fog poured from the pipe Norabel was smoking. The seven strutted and posed like Beauty Queens, cackling with noisy laughter all the

67

while, until Sybil minced over to Perry Logan, batting her ancient eyelashes.

'Er – your name please?' asked Perry. This wasn't quite what he expected, but the show must go on!

'Sybil Soreboils!'

'What a lovely name. And what is your ambition, Sybil?'

'To work with children,' said Sybil, squinting horribly.

'You're fond of children?'

'I love them – they're so *tasty,*' said Sybil, licking her lips. Then she let out a piercing cackle and added, 'I'm only kidding, folks!'

'This is much better than an ordinary beauty contest,' said Wendy. She laughed and laughed when Winifred said the person she'd most like to meet was Satan; and Peg said her hobby was turning television presenters into tadpoles, which seemed to upset Perry.

Wendy clapped and cheered, but the rest of the audience didn't seem to agree with her, for they'd all gone home. It was only then that Wendy thought of the time.

Back at home the Blue Witch was getting anxious. No sign of Wendy, and it was long past eleven o'clock!

'Something must have happened to her,' she fretted. 'I shouldn't have let her go alone, with Griselda on the loose.' She paced up and down

the floor. 'Sybil's very late too. I'll go out and look for them all. No, I'll stay, they might turn up any minute. No, I'll . . . oh, dear, I really can't make up my mind!'

There was a ring at the doorbell.

'Oh! Thank goodness, they've come,' she said, and rushed to the front door and opened it wide.

'Good morning,' said Griselda the Gruesome, reaching out her bony arms . . .

Wendy and her seven new friends soon came home. The little witch's heart sank to see the door left open and no sign of her old friend, except for a blue shawl lying on the mat.

'She's been kidnapped,' moaned Wendy when they'd searched the whole house. 'All because I left her on her own. Now Griselda's got her, that's the end of the Olympics for me! You've had a wasted journey, Sybil. The Blue Witch warned me herself – no more of your mischievous magic, she said. I forgot, and the worst has happend. It's all my fault.'

All afternoon they searched the town without finding the Blue Witch, and then they searched again till dusk, when they flew wearily home.

'You must be right,' said Sybil. 'I think Griselda *has* kidnapped her. A nasty piece of work, she is! When I was little at witch's school – I'm nearly as old as she is, you know – she was Head Girl. Once, for not polishing the broomsticks enough, she punished me with a week's boils on the bottom! I still remember it after five hundred years.'

'That's how Soreboils got her name!' cackled Winifred Wart.

'And that's why I'm joining your team,' said Sybil. 'To get my own back.'

'But there won't *be* a team without the Blue Witch,' Wendy pointed out tearfully.

'There is still *one* way to find out where she is,' said Sybil. 'The old, old way . . .'

'The smoke!' guessed Bathsheba, excited. 'But that needs at least eight witches over one hundred years old. And one of us hardly counts at all!'

Wendy was indignant. 'I've got my full Witch's Certificate, you know. And I'll try! I'll do anything to save the Blue Witch.'

'Then we'll have a go,' smiled Sybil. 'You'll really have to concentrate.'

The eight witches went into a huddle. Norabel puffed her pipe and the others, ignoring the awful smell, gazed into the rising smoke.

'I see something long, purple, and knob-bly . . .' droned Bathsheba.

'That's my nose, you fool!' hissed Norabel.

'Oh, so it is, sorry!'

'I see faces . . .' said Winifred Wart.

'Two cruel faces . . .' said Peg Pigbristle.

'Go on!' said Wendy, excited.

'I see an old woman tied up!' said Sybil. 'It's her, I'm sure it is!'

'I see trees through a window . . . lit by moonlight,' said Harriet Horsefeatures.

'Where, where?' said Wendy.

'It's no good, it's fading,' said Tabitha.

'Puff harder, Norabel. Make more smoke!' Wendy urged.

'I feel sick!' wailed Norabel. She did look awfully green! All the same, she puffed and puffed.

Winifred said, 'I see a board, with writing on . . . Visitors 237, Home Team 9 all out . . .'

Wendy said gleefully, 'That's it! The Willowdale Cricket Pavilion!'

The others stared at her. 'Why Willowdale? It could be anywhere.'

Wendy laughed. 'Nobody but the Willowdale cricket team gets bowled out for only nine runs! Come on – what are we waiting for?'

The witches climbed on their broomsticks and flew one by one out of an open window; except that little old Bathsheba's eyes were so full of smoke that she flew into the wall first time, and got tangled in the curtain next; but she made it at the third try.

In an hour they came triumphantly home with the Blue Witch, all laughing, and shrieking, and hugging each other in relief, until the neighbours banged on the walls for quiet.

'Easy! Easy!' chanted Harriet. 'Who'd have thought we'd catch Griselda and Malicious in the middle of an argument? Who'd have thought they'd turn each other into cricket balls just as we arrived?'

'Who'd have thought young Wendy would pick up a cricket bat and hit them both for six?' chortled Norabel. 'Right into the river!'

Just then some visitors called – the seven *real* finalists in the Beauty Contest, seven very cross girls.

'One of us would have been Miss Willowdale, but for you and your spell!' they told Wendy. They were so mad that before flouncing out of the house, each one gave Wendy a thump, right on her ear!

The witch moaned and clutched her ear. 'I suppose I deserve that. I've learned my lesson – no more bad magic!' But her eyes twinkled. 'Well, until after the Olympics, anyway!'

'Poor Wendy!' laughed Sybil, as they started to make plans for the Witch's Relay Race. 'These will cheer you up. I found them in the cricket pavilion.'

She handed Wendy the bunch of silver and blue balloons.

6 · The As-You-Were Potion . . .

The Blue Witch held races in the park, and
Norabel and Sybil were fastest. All agreed those
two should join the Relay. The others would
cheer the team on. At night Wendy, the Blue
Witch, the broomstick and Midnight went out
to practise the Hexathlon's last event, which
could only be done in secret on a fine moonlit
night.

The lost cricket balls at the bottom of the
river went to Vanishing Land. There (once
they'd turned back into Griselda and her
husband) they collected the enormous bat, and
rode it until its time came to burst back into the
real world – just the same way as people's lost
keys or glasses usually turn up in the end.

Since the kidnap plan had gone wrong the
dismal duo had been barely on speaking terms.
Griselda was sulking dreadfully. She'd have to
compete for her Gold Medal at the Games after
all! No chance to get at Wendy beforehand,
with all those witches about!

'Perhaps a little exercise?' Malicious suggested. 'We really ought to practise, you know.'

'Exercise? What, at my age?' squawked his wife. 'You must be joking! Anyway, that Belinda Witch may *start* the Hexathlon – but she won't be staying long!'

'She won't?'

Griselda gave her most sinister cackle. 'Not after she's drunk my As-You-Were Potion!'

'Never heard of it,' said Malicious.

'It's only the most powerful potion in the world! That's all! Why, one drop of it can turn Superman back into Clark Kent! It can unlaunch a ship! Unroast a turkey! Unshred a Shreddie! It can turn Wednesday back into Tuesday afternoon!'

'And what will it do to Wendy Witch?'

'One tiny sip – in a nice, refreshing bottle of, say, cherryade – and she'll turn back into a perfectly ordinary schoolgirl again! No more magic power, no more spells. The judges will disqualify her on the spot –'

'She'll be sent home in disgrace –'

'Leaving me the Gold Medal –'

'Back to school she'll have to go! Sums, and P.E. lessons, and homework!'

The terrible pair rocked with laughter until tears came to their eyes.

'Just what she deserves for daring to challenge you,' wheezed Malicious.

Griselda stopped laughing. 'The only problem is – I haven't got any.'

Malicious stopped laughing. 'Then we must get some!'

'Brilliant,' muttered Griselda. 'It's not so simple. There's only one place where the As-You-Were Potion can be found. It's a long and dangerous journey.'

The magician puffed out his chest. 'I, Malicious, will fetch it for you, wherever it may be!'

'Not you,' said Griselda. 'I've had enough of your bungling. Glenda Witch must be stopped! I shall go myself.'

Long past the witching hour of midnight, Griselda reached the foot of Witch's Hill. Knee-deep in the thick bracken, she moved hither and thither, searching; and at last came upon a slab of stone half-hidden under a hawthorn tree. Smiling, she strode away to circle the Witch's Hill no less than three times; and after the third time, she sank down upon the same stone and uttered strange words in a forgotten language. The stone slid aside. Griselda shone her torch. A tunnel led into the earth. She clambered in.

Swiftly the witch followed the twists and

turns of the passage, though at times it was narrow enough to touch her on both sides, until it opened into a wide, dripping cavern called the Cavern of Everloa. Here her footsteps echoed back at her as if a hundred Griseldas were hurrying through. Beyond, the tunnel plunged steeply so that the witch could barely keep her feet. When one wall of the tunnel dropped away, leaving Griselda only a narrow ledge, she knew she'd reached the Chasm of Yetdepa, where one slip could put an end to her plans by dashing her on to jagged rocks far below.

Still on she sped, leaving the Chasm far behind. On until she grew weary, her legs numb, and only the plod, plod, plodding of her own footsteps kept her awake; only the wickedness in her old bones drove her forward.

And only then came a regular drip, drip, dripping; and suddenly the tunnel ended at a murky pool rimmed with strange, twisted crystals. Needles of rock hung down above the pool, and from these, drops of liquid fell which shone with all the rainbow colours in the light of Griselda's torch. She had reached her goal: the Nobottom Well!

Griselda's eyes gleamed wickedly as she scooped up some of the syrupy rainbow drops into a flask.

The As-You-Were-Potion!

. . . and the Witch Olympics

At last the great day arrived. The Witch Olympics had begun. Wendy looked nervously round the stadium. It was full of cheering witches and wizards from all over the world.

'You can do it, Wendy!' the Blue Witch said as the Hexathlon was announced. 'Griselda's been champion long enough. I expect you've got a few butterflies in your tummy?'

Wendy gulped. 'I think it's a whole family of bats!'

Griselda the Gruesome arrived and did some warming-up exercises, running on the spot and touching her toes.

'No hard feelings about what's past, eh?' she said to Wendy. 'Honest, fair competition, that's the main thing now, isn't it? See – I brought you a present!' She handed Wendy a bottle of cherryade.

Wendy was touched by the thought. 'Thank you,' she said. 'Just what I need on this hot day. I'll have a drink right now!' She was just about to open the bottle when, to Griselda's secret annoyance, the Grey Wizard bustled up to start the competition.

Stopwatches, starting pistols, clipboards, rulebooks, *and* a hairdryer hung from the Grey Wizard's robe.

'I'm your referee for the Hexathlon. May the best witch win!' he said. 'The first event is the Broomstick Hurl. Take your places please! Griselda to hurl first.'

High up in his commentary box, Perry Logan spoke to millions watching on television: 'So here comes the defending champion,

Griselda. What a speed for a 571-year-old! This is just like the javelin, folks, only in the Witch Olympics you throw a broomstick instead. And *what* a throw it is! Well past the Grey Wizard's flag! You can hear the cheers. That'll be hard to beat. Now here comes Wendy Witch. Can she match the champion's throw?

'What's this? It can't be! It is – it's a giant wasp, big as a chicken, chasing Wendy along her run-up. Wendy's seen it, she's running faster. I have to tell you this – the wasp came from Griselda's gown. Yes, viewers, Griselda is cheating, trying to spoil the little witch's throw. The referee didn't see. Shame on you, Griselda! But will the trick work?

'Wendy's running like the wind, folks – no wonder, with that wasp after her! She's thrown her broomstick – and run off! Yes, she's streaked right off the field! See that throw – it hasn't come down yet, folks! Look at that. It's crossed the whole arena and landed in the crowd. Wendy wins! It's a stupendous Hurl!'

Perry Logan's voice was lost in cheers. He wiped his brow. The excitement was almost too much to bear.

'Well, everyone, that's one up to Wendy. The Blue Witch is fetching her back from the dressing room right now. Here she comes, still trembling. But it's all right, the wasp's gone – back up Griselda's sleeve, I shouldn't wonder.

And now for Event No. 2: the Toad-and-Spoon Race. You know the rules, ladies and gentlemen: if your toad jumps out of the spoon, it's back to the start you have to go! These Superstars of the Witch world would love a nice, relaxed, sleepy toad that would sit quietly in the spoon. But no such luck for them! All the toads you can see there in the Grey Wizard's barrel are specially changed for these Olympics – from the grumpiest, crosspatchiest school caretakers that could be found. Yes, you can see them now in close-up, grumbling and moaning away like mad.

'Now look at that! Did you see that, viewers? Behind the referee's back, Griselda actually changed her own husband into a toad and hid him up her sleeve. Did we get that on camera, Cecil? Great! And now she's pretending to dip in the barrel, but you can bet the toad she's pulled out is that slimy husband of hers.

'Now they're at the start. Wendy's toad is wriggling already. There's the starter's gun! Griselda's off like a shot – *her* toad's hanging on tight for fear of falling off. What did I tell you? It's Malicious all right. But Wendy's toad's hopped off! She's arguing with it, begging it to get back in the spoon. The toad is saying he's really a prince, and won't ride in a common spoon like hers. Nothing less than a silver spoon will do! This is tragic for the young contestant. And already it's all over! Griselda's finished the course, Wendy's still at the start arguing. The score is one all!'

Down in the arena, Griselda came over to Wendy. 'Bad luck, dear, to get such a stubborn toad! Here, have a refreshing drink of cherry-ade to cheer you up.'

'Not before the Relay,' replied the young witch. 'I couldn't run with all that fizz inside me!'

'Bother!' seethed Griselda. Would the wretched girl *never* take a drink?

'The Witch's Relay Race is next,' Perry Logan announced. 'This is a team event, ladies and gentlemen, and I hope we see no more of this cheating. Griselda's team, that's herself, Malicious, and two, well, they look like demons to me, with their arrow-tipped tails and glowing red eyes. Demons, Cecil? Cecil agrees. Wendy's team includes the Blue Witch, Sybil Soreboils, and Norabel Knockaknees smoking that famous pipe of hers. Now the Grey Wizard hands each team its baton. They're off!'

But soon Perry was too indignant to speak, when Griselda (waiting to run last) began casting spells on the other team's baton! As Norabel tried to hand it on to Sybil (in a cloud of smoke) it turned into a hissing snake. At the end of Sybil's lap it became so red-hot that the Blue Witch had to find a bucket of water to pour over it. And, as the Blue Witch tried to hand it on to Wendy, she couldn't let go, for the baton had mysteriously got coated with Superglue. They had to stagger round the last lap together. Of course Griselda's team had finished long ago! And worse was to come in the Witch's Cat Race.

'Wendy Witch hugs her little cat, Midnight, at the starting line,' Perry Logan told the world. 'But what's this? Is *that* Griselda's cat? Why, it's as big as a donkey! Surely this won't be allowed. Wendy's team has protested. The Grey Wizard's checking that enormous so-called cat; he's surely going to disqualify it. No! He's waved it on! This is unbelievable. The crowd are booing, and no wonder!'

But the race was on; and though Wendy changed her cat into a racehorse, an ostrich, and then a cheetah (as was allowed after the first lap), Griselda did the same – and *her* 'cat' (which had a distinct look of Griselda's enormous bat about it) was so much bigger, it outran Midnight from the start. Griselda didn't bother pretending to be friendly now.

'Three to me, one to you!' crowed Griselda. 'You can't beat me now!'

'But you're cheating!' glared Wendy. The old crone only cackled in wicked delight.

The fifth event in the Hexathlon was the Synchronized Broomstick Flying, in which two broomstick riders performed acrobatics in perfect time with each other. Points were given for technical merit and artistic impression, but the most important, the absolutely vital, essential thing was to KEEP SMILING at all times. Even when hanging upside down by one ankle at eighty miles an hour!

Griselda and Malicious gave a faultless performance. Their compulsory Double Axle

Grease was a wonder; and their Triple Backward Saltcellar made the crowd gasp. But though Griselda kept up an evil leer which passed for a smile, her partner spoiled it by scowling horribly all the way through because his broomstick had given him a painful splinter.

So here was a chance for Wendy to catch up.

She and the Blue Witch began well. They made several graceful broomstick-passes above the stadium, then a breathtaking Double Backward Swoop to the ground, pulling up sharply at the last moment. It was perfect. All that practising had paid off! The spectators sprang to their feet cheering.

But Griselda had a nasty surprise in store. While no one was looking she'd fixed a rocket to the Blue Witch's broom. It went off now with a stream of sparks, sending the Blue Witch zigzagging in all directions.

Wendy was thunderstruck. Then, filled with a fierce determination not to let Griselda's cheating beat her again, she yelled: 'Keep SMILING!' to the Blue Witch, and threw herself into a mad chase. She matched her partner turn for turn, twist for twist, and zig for zag, smiling for all she was worth in sheer excitement.

The Blue Witch dived, looped, and span at the mercy of the rocket; but Wendy kept up with every soar and swoop.

Never had the crowd seen such a thrilling performance! Surely such artistry could never be equalled! At last, the rocket spent, the two witches glided to earth as one, and sank flat to the ground. Their gowns billowed, then settled over the two still forms. After the first stunned silence came rapturous applause!

It was a triumph. The marks were excellent. Wendy had pulled up to three-two, and only the last event was left.

7 · 'Seventeen Times as High as the Moon'

Right on time the Grey Wizard announced the last event: the Old Woman Tossed-up-in-a-Basket Competition!

This was the climax of the day. It tested the magic skills of the contestants to the limit. In a basket not much bigger than a supermarket trolley, an Old Woman would be hurled far into space by magic powers alone. Spectators would see the action on the giant television screen looming over the stadium.

'Oho! It's the Hurl-a-Hag contest,' said the broomstick. 'I'm not in this. Can I go for a nice sandpaper rub-down?'

'No, you can't,' Wendy insisted. 'You've got to come and sweep cobwebs off the sky, remember? And Midnight's coming too, because she brings me luck. And don't be so rude! Hurl-a-Hag, indeed!'

These days the rules allowed a co-witch in the basket; so Wendy and the Blue Witch climbed into theirs, and Malicious clambered in with Griselda. It was a tight squash for the magician.

'What have you got in your bloomers, dear?' he said. 'They seem even more bulgy than usual!'

It was just beginning to get dark. The full moon was out, giving the contestants a target to aim for. Wendy mustered all her magic and said:

'Ancient powers of earth arise,
Bear us swiftly to the skies!'

The basket lifted off from the centre of the arena. Higher and higher it rose in eerie silence, lit by floodlights from below. The crowd, hushed, watched till it was only a speck high above. Then thousands of eyes swivelled to the giant screen, which now showed the second basket rising in pursuit.

When they were a mile high, strong winds gave the basket a tossing; at two miles, the Blue Witch took off her pointed hat, letting her hair stream out. Joy lit up her wrinkled face.

'Oh, this is a treat! It's the best ride of my life! It's a thrill! It's a wonder!'

Still Wendy worked hard, conjuring up the magic to take them past the Moon. Soon they were clear out in space. Only witchcraft kept them alive and breathing without spacesuits. A bird seemed to fly past. Impossible! Of course, it was only a Space Shuttle.

They passed the Moon and left it far behind, until the Earth was no bigger than a dark button against the stars, its rim lit up by the blazing sun beyond.

'Now, broomstick – brush the sky, collect cobwebs!'

'Don't be silly!' it snorted. 'There aren't any cobwebs in space!'

'Try it and see,' smiled the little witch. And it did; and there truly *were* cobwebs! The gossamer threads tumbled down into the basket, where Midnight gathered them into piles, and got them tangled round her whiskers. The wonderful sight of millions of stars made them feel it was all worthwhile, whatever the result.

And then it was time to return to earth, so Wendy began saying the charms that would carry them back. Suddenly there were whizzings and fizzings and thin shafts of cold pink light all about them.

'Oh! A shower of meteorites?' cried the Blue Witch in alarm. Wendy looked over the side of the basket.

'No, it's not,' she replied. 'Look down there.'

There below was Griselda's basket; and, in the old crone's hands, the ugly shape of a deadly laser wand! Beside her the magician had one too. Now they knew the reason for Griselda's bulgy bloomers!

'You can't do this!' called Wendy despairingly. 'Not out here! You mustn't spoil the peacefulness of space!'

'See if I can't,' cackled Griselda. The evil pair fired their weapons again, and Wendy's basket rocked, and shuddered, and span, until there was no sign of life inside.

'They'll never return to Earth, Malicious!' screamed the crone. 'No one will ever challenge me – the true Hexathlon Queen – ever again.'

Soon after, Griselda landed in the arena. The crowd searched the sky for the other basket, but there was no sign of it. The television screen was blank.

'They'll never return, I tell you!' screamed Griselda. 'I am the champion!'

'We'll wait a while,' said the Grey Wizard anxiously.

Wendy's basket was still on course, guided by the spells she'd cast. But its passengers never stirred. Soon Earth's gravity took hold, and sucked it down, faster and faster, towards a crash landing.

It was the Blue Witch who opened an eye and saw the Earth hurtling up towards her. At once she fingered some magic ingredients in her pocket and croaked:

'Oh, hemlock, bane, and mandrake root –
Let us down by parachute!'

And so it happened. Instead of smashing into the stadium, the basket drifted down by parachute to land with no more than a jolt, which woke the other stunned passengers. To Griselda's fury Wendy climbed out, shaken but unharmed.

'Now for the results,' said the Grey Wizard, shuffling his papers. 'Griselda reached a height of – let me see – seventeen times as high as the Moon!'

The crowd roared. 'That's a world record,' they agreed.

'Now for Wendy Witch's result. Wendy and the Blue Witch reached –' He waited for the crowd to be quiet. '– *nineteen* times as high as the Moon?'

Amid the clapping and cheering the Grey Wizard explained that the contestants had won three events each.

'It's a tie,' said Wendy gloomily. 'That means the champion will keep the title.'

But the panel of judges – the Ice Queen and the Green Wizard as well as the Grey Wizard – were arguing and checking the rule book. At last the small Green Wizard got up to speak. He turned red. Then he turned blue. Then, yellow and brown stripes.

'Sorry about this,' he said. 'I've been trying out a new colour-changing potion, and I spilt it down my robe.'

Everyone laughed. Just like the Green Wizard!

'The rule book is quite clear,' he went on. 'There are Bonus Points for the number of cobwebs brushed off the sky. The winner will be the witch with the most cobwebs.'

There was uproar. Everyone rushed to the baskets. Wendy proudly lifted out a fine heap of cobwebs, with Midnight fast asleep inside. The judges turned to Griselda. But she'd been too busy firing off her laser wand to remember the cobwebs. She hadn't got any!

Griselda the Gruesome stamped and fumed and screamed. She threw off her pointed hat and jumped on it. She boxed her husband about the ears. She boxed herself about the ears until her tongue stuck out and her eyes crossed.

'I can't believe it!' she raved. 'I've lost my medal! My Hexathlon Gold! It makes me so mad! It makes me wild! It makes me so . . . so THIRSTY!' The old witch gasped and spluttered and grabbed for the nearest drink – Wendy's bottle of cherryade, that stood on a trolley nearby – the one she'd put As-You-Were Potion in . . . She took an enormous, greedy swig.

Before their astonished eyes her evil face

changed; her witch's robes dropped away; and in a twinkling, there stood a kindly little old lady with grey hair and a shawl.

She took her husband's arm and said pleasantly, 'Come on, dear. It's been *such* an

94

exciting day, but I'd like to go home now.'

She patted Wendy on the arm in a grand-motherly way. 'Well done, dear. I hope you'll enjoy being champion. You did very well!'

She toddled off arm in arm with her husband to find a taxi.

'I'd just like to get my slippers on in front of the fire,' they could hear her saying. 'Isn't it *Crimewitch* on television tonight?'

So all that remained was for Wendy Witch to be given her Gold Medal, to everyone's delight; to say goodbye to Sybil and her friends and thank them for all they'd done; and, later, to set off home with the Blue Witch, on the way to a hero's welcome in Willowdale, where everyone had watched the contest on television. As they flew high over the busy motorway, they sang happily the old rhyme:

'There was an old woman tossed up in a basket
Seventeen times as high as the moon!
Where she was going, I couldn't but ask it
For in her hand she carried a broom.
Old woman, old woman, old woman, said I,
Where are you going to, up so high?
To brush the cobwebs off the sky!
May I go with you!
Aye, by and by.'

'Aye, by and by!' echoed the broomstick.
'Miaow!' sang Midnight.